RAPUNZEL

Rapunzel

Retold and illustrated by

Alix Berenzy

Henry Holt and Company ✦ New York

For Marcelle

—A.B.

Henry Holt and Company, Inc., *Publishers since 1866*
115 West 18th Street / New York, New York 10011

Henry Holt is a registered
trademark of Henry Holt and Company, Inc.

Copyright © 1995 by Alix Berenzy
All rights reserved.
Published in Canada by Fitzhenry & Whiteside Ltd.,
195 Allstate Parkway, Markham, Ontario L3R 4T8.

Library of Congress Cataloging-in-Publication Data
Berenzy, Alix.
Rapunzel / Alix Berenzy.
Based on the original German story.
Summary: A retelling of the German folktale in which a beautiful girl
with long golden hair is kept imprisoned in a lonely tower by a witch.
[1. Fairy tales.   2. Folklore—Germany.]   I. Title.
PZ8.B4477Rap   1995   398.2'0943'01—dc20   94-48941

ISBN 0-8050-1283-4
First Edition—1995
Calligraphy by Patricia Weisberg
Printed in the United States of America
on acid-free paper. ∞
1   3   5   7   9   10   8   6   4   2

The artist used colored pencil and gouache
on black paper to create the illustrations for this book.

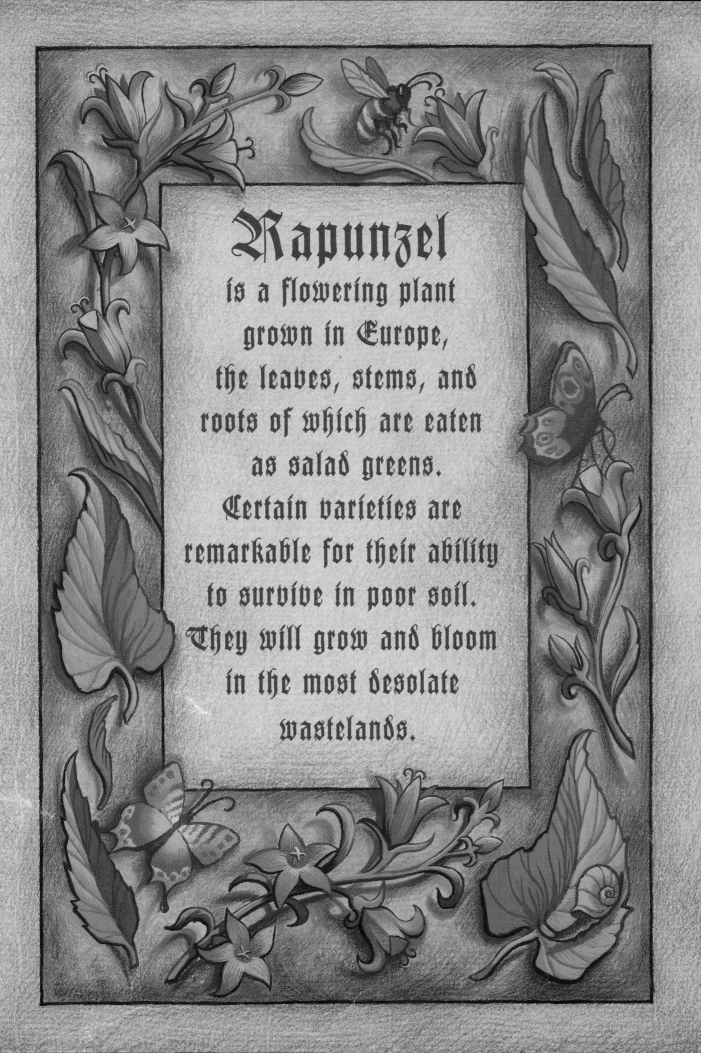

Rapunzel

is a flowering plant
grown in Europe,
the leaves, stems, and
roots of which are eaten
as salad greens.
Certain varieties are
remarkable for their ability
to survive in poor soil.
They will grow and bloom
in the most desolate
wastelands.

 LONG TIME AGO, in a little German town, a husband and wife hoped to have a child. At long last, their wish was to be granted.

At the back of the house was a small window and from it could be seen a beautiful garden. The garden belonged to an ancient fairy named Mother Gothel, and it was filled with the most wonderful flowers and herbs. Often the wife would pause at the window and gaze out at the garden.

She would watch the flowers as they swayed in the breeze. Butterflies danced in the sun and birds sang. With a sigh, she would return to her duties.

One beautiful summer day the wife stood again at the window. She was watching the bees humming among the blossoms when she spotted a magnificent flower bed of rapunzel. Suddenly, a great desire swept over her.

"I *must* taste some of that rapunzel," she said to herself. But, alas, she knew that she never would, for the garden was surrounded by a high stone wall and no one dared to enter. Everyone feared Mother Gothel's great powers.

The wife tried to forget about the rapunzel, but every day her desire grew stronger. Soon, no other food appealed to her, and she became weak and sickly.

Her husband was alarmed.

"What ails thee?" he asked.

"Oh," she sighed. "I crave that rapunzel in the garden. I fear I will die if I cannot taste it."

The husband did not want his wife to perish. He decided to get her the rapunzel, cost him what it may.

So that evening, he crept over the wall of the garden. Hastily he tore out a handful of rapunzel and escaped back home with it.

His wife was overjoyed! She made it into a big salad and ate every bite. It was so good she dreamed of it that night: in her dream rapunzel grew up all around the house and she could have as much as she wanted. But the next day the only rapunzel she could see lay out of reach in the fairy's garden. Though she felt stronger, stronger too was her desire for the plant. Soon, she was pale and weak again.

So once again at twilight, her husband crept over the garden wall. Only this time, as he was reaching for the plant, he saw a blinding flash of light and there stood Mother Gothel.

"How dare you steal my rapunzel!" she shouted. She fixed an angry eye upon him. "You will suffer for it," she snarled.

"Have mercy!" he cried. "My wife stands every day at the window looking at your garden. So great is her desire for rapunzel, I fear she will die unless she can have some!"

The fairy considered this. "I see how it is," she said. "I will let you take all the rapunzel you need to make her strong again—but on one condition. You must give me the baby that your wife is soon to bear. No harm will come to it. Indeed, I will care for it like a mother and protect it from the harsh ways of the world. The baby will be fortunate."

In his terror, the man agreed to everything.

IN TIME, the wife gave birth to a baby girl and the fairy appeared soon after to claim the child. She gave her the name Rapunzel and took her away.

APUNZEL grew to be an unusually beautiful child. She was gentle and innocent. Her hair shone like gold and grew wondrously long.

The fairy built the walls of the garden higher and allowed Rapunzel to play within them. But when Rapunzel was twelve years old, the fairy took her deep into the woods and locked her in a high tower. It had neither staircase nor door, just one little window at the top. Whenever Mother Gothel wished to visit the girl, she stood at the foot of the tower and cried out, "Rapunzel, Rapunzel, let down your hair for me."

Rapunzel obeyed by wrapping her long braids around a hook at the side of the window and letting them fall to the ground. The fairy fastened herself to them and Rapunzel pulled her up. So it went for many years and Rapunzel grew lonely, hidden away from the world.

But Rapunzel learned to sing. She made up beautiful songs and let her sweet voice ring out into the wilderness. The sound of her own voice lightened her heart and helped to fill the solitary hours.

NE SPRING DAY while the King's son was riding through the forest, he heard a lovely song carried on the wind. He was curious and followed the sound deep into the woods, where he came upon a forbidding tower. From it came a voice so sweet he stood there entranced.

The Prince searched in vain for a way into the tower. At last he became frustrated and rode away. But he found himself returning the next day, and every day after. Rapunzel's song had touched his heart.

Once, as he stood listening well-hidden behind a tree, he saw the fairy appear at the foot of the tower. He spied on her as she called up to the window, "Rapunzel, Rapunzel, let down your hair for me."

Two golden braids came tumbling down. The fairy fastened herself to them and was pulled up. She disappeared inside.

"Aha!" he said with a grin. "So *that* is the way to the bird's nest."

The next evening the Prince went to the foot of the tower, eager for adventure. He was careful to repeat exactly the words that the fairy had spoken, "Rapunzel, Rapunzel, let down your hair for me."

The braids came down at once. The Prince fastened himself to them and was pulled up.

When Rapunzel saw the Prince stepping through the window, she was terrified, for she had never set eyes on a man before. But the Prince spoke to her in a gentle way and she soon lost her fear of him. They talked together day after day. Rapunzel was overjoyed to have a companion, and the Prince was equally delighted with her. At last he said, "Will you be my wife? We can ride away together on my horse."

Rapunzel hesitated. The Prince was young and handsome and she had long wished to leave the tower. Still, she did not know him well. She needed to be sure he loved her truly and would not lock her away as Mother Gothel had done. A plan came to her.

"I will gladly be your wife," she said, as she laid her hand in his. "But I cannot get down from this tower. If you visit me every day and each time bring me a skein of silk, I will weave it into a ladder. When it is finished, I will descend by it and ride away with you."

Rapunzel cautioned him, "Come only in the evening as Mother Gothel comes in the daytime." To this the Prince agreed.

So every evening the Prince brought a skein of silk and as the ladder grew, so did their love. Soon, the ladder was almost finished, and Mother Gothel suspected nothing.

But one day Rapunzel forgot herself. "How is it, Mother Gothel, that you are harder to draw up than the Prince?" she asked. "Oh!" She clapped her hands over her mouth.

In that instant, the fairy knew she had been betrayed.

"I protected you from the world and yet you have deceived me!" she cried. She seized a pair of scissors and—*snip, snap*—Rapunzel's golden braids fell to the floor. With a hardened heart, she dragged Rapunzel far away to a barren and wasted desert and left her to fend for herself.

Rapunzel wept in fear as the
flowers fell from her hair.

HAT VERY EVENING, Mother Gothel fastened the severed braids to the window hook. She sat in the dark tower and waited.

Soon, the Prince appeared with the last skein of silk. He called out, "Rapunzel, Rapunzel, let down your hair for me."

The braids were lowered at once and the Prince was pulled up, eager to see his beloved Rapunzel.

Instead he found the fairy!

"You rogue!" she cried. "Your days of careless pleasure are over. The little songbird is gone. You will never see Rapunzel again!"

The Prince could not bear to hear these words and in despair jumped from the window. He fell into a thornbush and was blinded.

OW the Prince wandered about in darkness. He could do nothing but weep and grieve for the loss of his dear wife. He learned to live on roots and berries and over time his fine clothes turned to rags.

Years passed. Then one day he came to a strange windswept land. He heard a distant voice, singing. Could it be? He hurried toward the sound.

Yes, Rapunzel had survived! In terrible poverty she had given birth to twins, a girl and a boy, and done her best to feed and shelter them.

All around her, tiny rapunzel plants had sprouted and grown up in the harsh wasteland.

Rapunzel saw the Prince approaching. Though he had changed, she knew him at once and flew into his arms weeping with joy. Two of her tears fell upon his eyes and they were healed.

Now he saw Rapunzel's face and their two beautiful children. He saw the home she had made and the desert blooming with flowers.

Rapunzel and the Prince were filled with gratitude.

They swept the children into their arms. Together, they were able to find their way back to his kingdom, where the people rejoiced to see them and their return was celebrated with the greatest joy. As the years passed, their time was spent among friends and their hearts were filled with love. So their days together were happy indeed.